The Faithful Sister

The Faithful Sister

and other classic fairy-tales

Retold by Fiona Waters

Illustrated by
Gail Newey

BLOOMSBURY
CHILDREN'S
BOOKS

For Lizzie, with much love

First published in Great Britain in 2000
Bloomsbury Publishing Plc, 38 Soho Square, London, W1V 5DF

Copyright © Text Fiona Waters 2000
Copyright © Illustrations Gail Newey 2000

The moral right of the author has been asserted
A CIP catalogue record of this book is available from the
British Library

ISBN 0 7475 4704 1

Printed in England by Clays Ltd, St Ives plc

10 9 8 7 6 5 4 3 2 1

Contents

The Three Sisters

A story from Germany

There once lived a wealthy merchant
whose wife had long since died,
leaving him three daughters to bring
up. The eldest was called Armynel
and she was a cold, haughty
creature. Her skin was as white as
new fallen snow while her hair was

as black as a crow's wing. She walked proudly, and always dressed in the finest clothes. Sylvia was the second daughter and she was a flibbertigibbet. She was always laughing, and she danced everywhere with her hair flying, her dresses covered in ribbons and bows, but she was careless and thoughtless. The third girl, Freda, was gentle as her mother had been and quite overshadowed by her two sisters. She dressed simply in a white dress with blue smocking, her golden hair tied back in a thick plait, her face a mass of freckles like a bird's egg.

One dreadful day, the merchant fell
ill and not even the most expensive

apothecary could cure him. Now in the woods outside the town there was a magic spring and it was said that water from this spring could cure any ailment. The girls resolved to give their poor father some of this water. Armynel put on her finest

silks and brocades, took a heavy
silver jug down from the dresser
and swept off to the woods. No
sooner had she filled the jug than
with a terrible shout an awful
monster appeared by her side.

'Who said you could help yourself

to my water?' roared the Monster.

Armynel looked at the Monster in
horror for he really was very ugly.
He had matted green hair hanging
in fronds around his face and his
green teeth were sharp and pointed.

He was covered in coarse fur and he had webbed feet and fingers.

'I have come to fetch water for my father who is very ill. Stand aside and let me pass,' Armynel said haughtily.

But the Monster just grinned, showing all his terrible green pointed teeth.

'You can only have that jug of water if you will agree to marry me and live with me in my mossy cave,' he said softly.

'I wouldn't dream of marrying you!' said Armynel. 'You are far too ugly.'

'Ah, I thought not,' said the

Monster, still grinning. 'It is not right that such a fine lady as yourself should have to travel home on foot. I will lend you one of my finest horses.'

Before she knew it, there stood the most magnificent coal black horse pawing the ground. All thoughts of her poor father and the magical water gone, Armynel sprang up into the saddle, but she very soon realised that she could not control the huge beast who galloped faster and faster through briar thickets, across the river and down the muddy streets right to her own front door where it threw her headfirst in the dust. Her fine clothes were torn to shreds, her hair was tangled, her hands were dirty – and she had no precious water for her father.

The very next day, Sylvia decided
she would fetch the water for her
father. She just laughed when
Armynel told her to beware of the
Monster and put on her prettiest
dress covered in ribbons and
spangles. She took a fine Venetian

glass wine jug for the water. No
sooner had she filled the jug than
the Monster appeared just as before.

'You may have as much water as
you need for your father if you will
only marry me and live with me in
my mossy cave,' he said softly.

Sylvia just laughed and laughed, and twirled round in front of the Monster, her ribbons and spangles flying in the sunlight.

'Ah, I thought not,' said the Monster, grinning. 'But perhaps you would like to dance with the West Wind himself!'

And with that Sylvia was swept along by a huge gust of wind, all thoughts of her father and the magical water blown like swansdown from her thoughts. But the wind led her a merry dance through the trees, over the hedges and round the haystacks until it deposited her with a bump on her

own doorstep. Her clothes were snagged, her ribbons dusty and her spangles crushed – and she had no precious water for her father.

The next day, Freda fetched a brown earthenware jug from the kitchen and followed the path her

two sisters had taken into the
woods. When she reached the magic
spring the Monster was lying asleep
by the edge of the pool. She
carefully walked round him and
was filling the jug when she heard a
voice behind her saying softly,

'You may have as much water as you wish for your father if you will only marry me and live with me in my mossy cave.'

Freda turned round and looked at the Monster. He really was very ugly indeed. But her beloved father was dying so she smiled bravely at him and said,

'I will gladly marry you if your water will cure my father.'

'Ah, I thought so,' said the Monster, grinning from ear to ear and showing all his sharp green teeth.

He sprinkled her hair and her dress with water and in a shimmer

all the drops of water turned to
pearls. Then he sprinkled some
water on three pebbles and there
before Freda's astonished eyes was a
shining carriage drawn by two
white horses with their reins all

encrusted with mother-of-pearl and silver.

'Go to your father,' said the Monster. 'I will follow shortly,' and he dived deep into the pool.

Freda climbed into the carriage and went home to her father. As soon as she entered his room, a soft sweet breeze stole in through the open window. His eyes opened and the colour came back into his cheeks. Freda poured him a glass of the magical water and he drained it in one draught. He threw back the bedclothes and stood before her, smiling and fully restored to health.

Freda took her father by the hand

and sat him in the garden with a cooling glass of cordial. The birds were singing and the perfume from all the flowers was glorious and for a moment she put aside her fears about her rash promise to the Monster. But then she heard a

strange sound, a slapping noise on the flagstones in the kitchen, and suddenly there stood the Monster looking unbelievably ugly. Freda explained the bargain to her father. He was horrified at the thought of his gentle daughter with this awful

creature, but he too acknowledged that she had made a promise that couldn't be broken.

The Monster said quietly to Freda,

'Before we set off together perhaps you would give me a bath?'

Freda thought it strange that so dreadful a creature should think of washing, but none the less she fetched down the tin bath from the outhouse wall and filled it with warm water and some sweet-smelling herbs from her garden for the Monster smelt very dank. He stepped into the bath and Freda began to pour the water over him. To her astonishment, wherever the

water touched him, his terrible skin
began to slough away and there
stood the most handsome man, all
dressed in sea green silk. He
stepped out of the bath and kissed
Freda gently on the cheek, saying,
    'Now come with me to the pool

again, and you shall see the mossy
cave where we must live together.'

Freda's spirits sank again but
when they reached the pool all was
changed and there stood a gorgeous
palace with wonderful gardens full
of fountains and statues of sea

creatures. Freda and her father and her handsome husband all lived together happily for the rest of their days. And what of the two mean sisters, Armynel and Sylvia? They were so consumed with annoyance and jealousy that they quite lost their good looks and became two very crabby old maids!

The Faithful Sister

A story from India

There was once a sister and brother
who were as close as close can be.
Madhavi loved her little brother,
Rahul, with all her heart but soon it
was time for her to be married
herself and as her new husband
lived a long way away she didn't

see very much of her precious
brother. Madhavi had children of
her own, but she never forgot her
dearest darling brother. He grew up
too and soon it was time for him to
be married.

'I do so want my sister to be at

my wedding,' Rahul said to his parents. 'Please may I take her an invitation myself in plenty of time for her to make the journey here,' for in those far off times travelling took many, many weeks.

Madhavi was overjoyed to be

reunited with her brother and to receive the invitation. After bidding her husband a fond farewell, for he was a good man, Rahul and Madhavi set off at once on their long journey.

They travelled for many days and were hot and dusty and tired. They saw a well in the distance and agreed they would stop for a rest and a drink. Rahul threw himself down on the ground and was soon in a deep sleep, so exhausted was he. Madhavi went on down to the well and had just drawn herself a long cool beaker of water when she saw an old man sitting in the shade

of some trees by the well. He
looked utterly weary so she called
over to him,

'Good sir, may I fetch you some
water?'

The old man raised his head and
she saw that his eyes were milky
with blindness. He turned towards
her with a smile and said,

'Thank you, daughter. I should be very glad of refreshment.'

He drank long from the beaker and turned again to Madhavi.

'And is that your brother lying asleep yonder?' he asked.

Now Madhavi wondered greatly at this question for how could the old man know her brother was there when he was so obviously blind?

'He is indeed, but how . . .?' she started to ask, but the old man put his hand on her sleeve and smiled gently.

'I am a prophet. It is my task in life to help people whenever I can.

And I have to tell you your brother is in great need of help. Unless you do just as I say he will be dead within a day of his wedding.'

Well, Madhavi was terrified by this. Here was her dearest brother on the brink of his new life with his chosen bride and now he was apparently doomed. She wept and wrung her hands and pleaded with the prophet,

'Surely this cannot be! My brother has led a blameless life and is a kind and gentle man. Why have the gods so chosen to destroy our happiness?'

'It is not for us to question the

ways of the gods, my child,' said
the old man. 'But do not despair
utterly. Your brother can be spared
but only through the great love of
his sister.'

'Tell me, tell me what I have to do. He is my beloved only brother and I would do anything to save him!' pleaded Madhavi.

'It will not be easy,' said the old man. 'You will have to pretend to be mad. You must utterly convince

everyone, most of all your brother. You must shed all your graceful behaviour and your modesty, and, no matter what is said or done to you, you must not waver from this course of action. You must maintain this pretence until your brother's

new bride has been under his roof
for one full day and night. Only
then will your brother be saved.'

'I will do anything to save my

brother,' Madhavi vowed and she kissed the old man's hand and thanked him for showing her a way she might save Rahul.

She walked slowly towards her still sleeping brother, looking over her shoulder once only to discover that the prophet had vanished.

And so began her great trial. First she rolled in the dust, then she tore her beautiful sari and then she began howling and shrieking. Rahul awoke with a great start to be confronted with the sight of his sister rolling around like a dervish and shrieking like a madwoman.

'Madhavi, what is the matter with

you?' he cried and tried to pacify
her.

But she only shrieked all the more
and began to call him all kinds of
rude names.

'You idiot! You son of a donkey!
Your mother is a monkey and your
father a baboon!' she yelled.

Rahul thought he had awakened
to a nightmare. Only a little while
back his sister had been calling him
her dearest darling and now here
she was behaving like a madwoman.

'My sister, you have gone mad!'
he cried.

'Oh ho! Mad is it? You are the one who is mad. Going off to marry that ugly pig of a bride. Come on we must hurry. You can't be late for your dreadful wedding,' and so saying she dragged him off down the road.

Rahul was bewildered. He thought it best to keep silent and to wait and see what happened when they reached his home. And so they journeyed, he with head cast down in embarrassment, she cursing and swearing like a fishwife. People on the road looked in amazement at the pair, many suggesting that he get his sister locked up as soon as

possible for she was clearly mad as
a jackass.

When they finally arrived home
their mother came running to meet

them but was horrified when her
daughter took one look at her and
said,

'Who is this ugly old nanny
goat?'

Rahul explained that all had been
well until they were halfway home

and then Madhavi had suddenly
gone crazy.

'What are we going to do?' he
asked. 'She will ruin my wedding.
Whatever will my bride's family
think?'

The wedding day came. As all the

important guests began to arrive, Madhavi could be heard yelling and screaming. The bride's parents began to wonder if they had made a dreadful mistake in arranging the marriage.

Madhavi was muttering all through the ceremony but just as the wedding crown was about to be placed on her brother's head she rushed up and dashed it to the ground. There was a loud gasp as a viper slid out on to the tiled floor.

'Well, my sister may be mad but I think she has just saved my life,' murmured Rahul.

The bridal procession slowly

made its way down the village
street and was about to pass under
the ceremonial gates when
Madhavi began yelling again.

'I want to ride at the head of the
procession. It is not right that I am
left here at the back!'

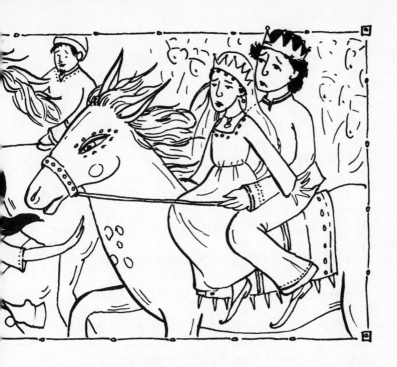

Rahul just wanted his
embarrassment to be over so he
asked everyone to let his sister
through to the front, but while they
were all trying to sort themselves
out there was a great crash. The
main arch of the gateway had

collapsed in a cloud of dust.

'Well, my sister may be mad but I think she has just saved my life,' murmured Rahul.

They finally all arrived at the splendid new home Rahul had built for his new bride. No sooner had they all dismounted than Madhavi began wailing and shrieking again. By this time the bride's parents were planning to bundle their daughter up and steal her away as fast as possible for clearly she had married into a family of lunatics.

Madhavi demanded to be allowed to sleep in the bridal chamber.

'Get out, all of you. I must sleep in that bed not that pig of a brother of mine and his old crone of a wife!'

But just as she lay down on the petal strewn bed a huge scorpion scuttled across the sheets.

'Well, my sister may be mad but I think she has just saved my life,' murmured Rahul.

No one slept very well that night. The new bride was weeping, her parents were arguing furiously with Rahul's parents and Madhavi,

of course, was cursing and raving
in the cellar where Rahul had
finally been forced to lock her.

The next day Rahul said to his
parents,

'What are we to do with
Madhavi? She cannot stay here. I

think we must get her back to her husband as fast as possible.'

His mother looked sadly at the beautiful golden sari she had bought for Madhavi to wear at the wedding.

'I might as well give this away. She will never wear it now,' but as she spoke a calm voice came from the cellar.

'Let me out, my dearest brother. I am restored to my own self.'

It was Madhavi. A full day and night had passed since the new bride had been under her brother's roof and she was free to tell her tale.

'Only by pretending to be mad
could I persuade you to let me
behave so badly that I might be

there to protect you wherever you were.'

Rahul held her close and said to everyone,

'But for my beloved sister I would be dead. I am twice blessed to have

a sister who not only loves me but who was prepared to lose her good name and reputation to save me. I thank you, dearest Madhavi, with all my heart.'

Great was the rejoicing, and they

decided to celebrate the wedding all over again. Madhavi wore the beautiful golden sari – and this time there were no interruptions!

Two Sisters and the Snake

A story from China

There was once a hard-working old woman who had been widowed very young. She had two daughters; the elder was lazy and selfish while the younger was kind and looked after her mother well.

One day as the mother was

returning from working in the rice fields she sat down under a mango tree to rest her weary back. The smell of the ripe mangoes made her mouth water but she dared not pick one as the tree did not belong to

her. Suddenly she was showered with bits of bark from the tree, but when she looked up she couldn't see anyone there. She brushed the bark off her lap and leaned back against the tree again. Once more

she was suddenly covered with bits
of bark and this time, without even
looking up, she said aloud,

'Whoever you are, if you are kind enough to give me one of those delicious mangoes, I will give you one of my daughters in marriage.'

She was only joking, of course, but the words were no sooner out of her mouth than her lap was full of sweet ripe mangoes. Now the old woman was very frightened for she suspected that there was magic afoot. She sprang to her feet and peered up into the branches of the tree and her heart went cold. For there coiled round the trunk of the tree was a very large snake!

Scattering the mangoes in her haste, the old woman ran off home

as fast as she could go and locked
the door behind her very securely.

'Dearest Mother,' said the
younger sister, 'whatever is the
matter? Sit quietly here and calm
yourself, you are quite safe. I will
look after you.'

'Alas, my daughters, I have not
looked after you very well,' said
the old woman and she told them
about her encounter with the snake.

Well, the elder sister flew into a
huge rage and stormed round the
room shouting and tearing her hair.

'How could you be so stupid!' she yelled. 'I am certainly not going to be married off to a snake.'

The younger sister gave her mother a drink of jasmine tea and soothed her.

'I am sure nothing will happen, Mother dearest. Perhaps it was all just a dream.'

But when she looked out of the window there was a huge snake coiled round the gatepost. She took a lantern and went down the path and just as she was about to turn and run away, for it was a very big snake, it spoke to her.

'Your mother made a promise to

me that I should have one of her daughters in marriage. Are you here to keep that promise?'

The younger daughter had no desire whatsoever to be married to a snake any more than her elder sister, but she knew a promise

was a promise, however lightly given, and she did not want to distress her mother any more. She said to the snake,

'I will honour my mother's promise to you.'

And with tears in her eyes she followed the

snake as it slithered off into the
forest. The elder sister was
watching through the open door
and as soon as her sister and the
snake had disappeared, she

slammed the door shut and said to her weeping mother,

'Let that be a lesson to you for your greed!'

She was not a nice person but the story is not finished yet.

The younger sister and the snake went deep into the forest where even the moon did not shine. As they went the girl wept bitter tears but the snake never turned its head or stopped.

Ever deeper into the forest they went and then into a dark and gloomy cave.

The girl wept even more as they passed into such utter darkness

that she could not even see her
hand before her face. Then the
snake stopped so suddenly that she
bumped into it and felt the long
scaly coils and as she smothered a
scream she heard the snake say,

'Dry your eyes for there is much

to see!' and there was a great glow
of warm light. There in front of her
the girl saw a magnificent palace.
Great shining dragons of gold
guarded the gates. Shady
courtyards were filled with willow
trees, and ponds sparkled with

silver and golden carp. The soaring wooden ceilings were painted in rich blues and reds, and tapestries hung over the railings. Rainbow silks blew gently in the breeze and statues of carved jade stood in tiled niches. Music played gently in the background and the air was filled with the scent of blossom. The younger sister was astonished and turned to look for the snake. Even more astonishment! Where the snake had been there now stood a handsome young man dressed in great finery. He bowed very low and spoke to the girl, and his voice was rich and warm.

'I am the King of the Snakes and I wish you to be my Queen. I have watched you as you looked after your mother, I have seen your gentle ways and I admire your kindness. I promise to look after you for ever and you will lack for nothing.'

And the younger sister cried again, but this time her tears were of joy and they fell as pearls about her feet. She took the Snake King's hand and walked into the palace with him and they were married amid great rejoicing.

After a few days, she begged to

be allowed to return to her mother
to tell her how happy she was. The
Snake King was reluctant to let her
go, but he could see she would not
be happy until she had put her

mother's mind at rest. He took her
to the entrance of the cave and bid
her a safe journey, making her
promise she would return within
four days. She ran all the way
through the forest until she reached
her old home and there was her
mother, standing by the gate. They
both cried with joy at seeing each
other again and sat for hours
drinking tea while the younger
sister told her wondering mother
all about the Snake King and his
fabulous palace. Her mother was
overjoyed at her daughter's good
fortune but her elder sister was
consumed with jealousy and began

to regret her haste in refusing to marry the snake. She was not a nice person but the story is not finished yet.

When the younger sister returned to her husband the King, the elder sister came with her. As she saw all

the tiled verandas and rich
pavilions with peacocks strutting
round, and ate off the golden plates
at the King's table her jealousy
knew no bounds. Promising the
younger sister that she would look
after their mother, she ran off into

the forest as fast as possible. She had no intention of returning to her mother and their humble home but was determined to find a snake she could marry as soon as possible.

'There are plenty of snakes in the forest. I will catch one and we can be married. Then I will live even better than my sister,' she vowed.

She searched all day in vain but just as the light was fading she found a huge snake fast asleep under a tree. She quickly stuffed the snake into a basket and set off to arrange the marriage ceremony. But the snake had been enjoying a good sleep and was very angry at

being disturbed, and was even more angry at being stuffed so unceremoniously into the basket.

It pushed open the lid of the basket and before the elder sister realised what was happening the snake had swallowed her whole!

Now the King of the Snakes saw all this happening for his magical powers were very great and he resolved to teach the elder sister a lesson. He summoned the snake with the sister inside to the palace and he also sent a messenger for

the poor old mother who was sitting sadly at home all alone. The snake arrived, with its sides bulging, and the mother arrived, quite overwhelmed at the speed of her journey and the richness of her surroundings.

All the courtiers were present as the King called out in a very loud voice,

'Let that be a lesson to you for your greed!' the very words the elder daughter had used so heartlessly against her own mother.

To the astonishment of everyone a muffled reply came from inside the snake, for in its rage it had

swallowed the girl alive.

'I will never again be so selfish if
only you will rescue me from inside
here.'

The Snake King took the bulging
snake into a small room to one side
and spoke privately to it and

seconds later the elder sister was kneeling at the feet of her mother, begging her forgiveness. The younger sister was delighted to see her sister fully restored and asked her husband if both she and their mother might stay with them in the gorgeous palace. Because he loved

his wife, the King readily agreed to her request but because he never quite trusted the elder sister, he appointed the no longer bulging, but still rather cross, snake to stand guard outside her door lest she slip back into her old ways. And the generous King always made sure the old mother had a fresh supply of ripe and juicy mangoes every day!